HO 8/05 E
HEA

Inside Me, Sometimes

Library of congress cataloging-in-publication data

Heath, Gail, 1947-
    Inside Me Sometimes / written and illustrated by Gail Heath.
        P.   cm.
    Summary: A whimsical octopus portrays contrasting
emotions and invites readers to see those feelings in themselves.
    ISBN 1-56763-312-9 (cloth : alk Paper). — ISBN 1-56763-
313-7 (paper : alk. paper)
    [1. Emotions—Fiction. 2. Octopus—Fiction.] I. Title
PZ7.H3475In   1998
[E]—dc20   96-42000
                                                           CIP
                                                           AC

Printed in the United States of America

Inside Me, Sometimes

Written and illustrated by

Gail Heath

Ozark Publishing, Inc.
P.O. Box 228
Prairie Grove, AR 72753

Dedicated with love to John E., Jason, and Sara, who are like this sometimes.

Foreword

A whimsical octopus portrays contrasting emotions and then invites young readers to see those feelings in themselves.

Sometimes I am so happy
that I bounce like a bunny, or

I am so sad that I cry a pail full of
tears.

Sometimes I am so brave that I invite a ghost to tea, or

3

I am so scared that a butterfly
can make me run.

Sometimes I am so
friendly that I kiss a frog, or

I am so lonely that I dance with
my shadow.

Sometimes I am so nice that I take my little brothers and sisters for a walk, or

I am so mean that I pull the
petals off a daisy.

Sometimes I am so big that
I climb over buildings, or

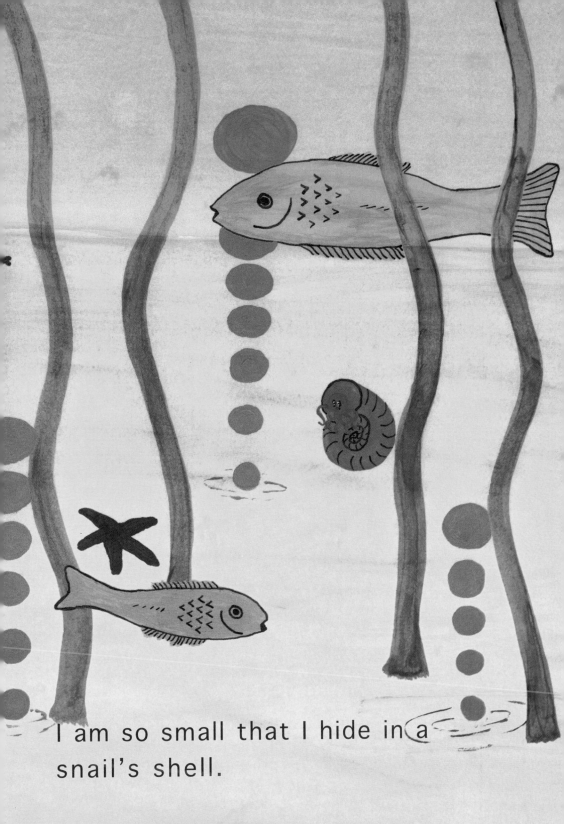

I am so small that I hide in a snail's shell.

Sometimes I am so generous
that I share my treasure with
my friends, or

I am so selfish that I take my toys and go home.

Sometimes I am so proud
that I almost pop, or

I am so ashamed that I hide my head.

Sometimes I am so clever
that I read to myself, or

I am so silly that I wear
socks for mittens.

Sometimes I am so cheerful
that I float like a bunch of
balloons, or

I am so angry that I kick a
tree.

20

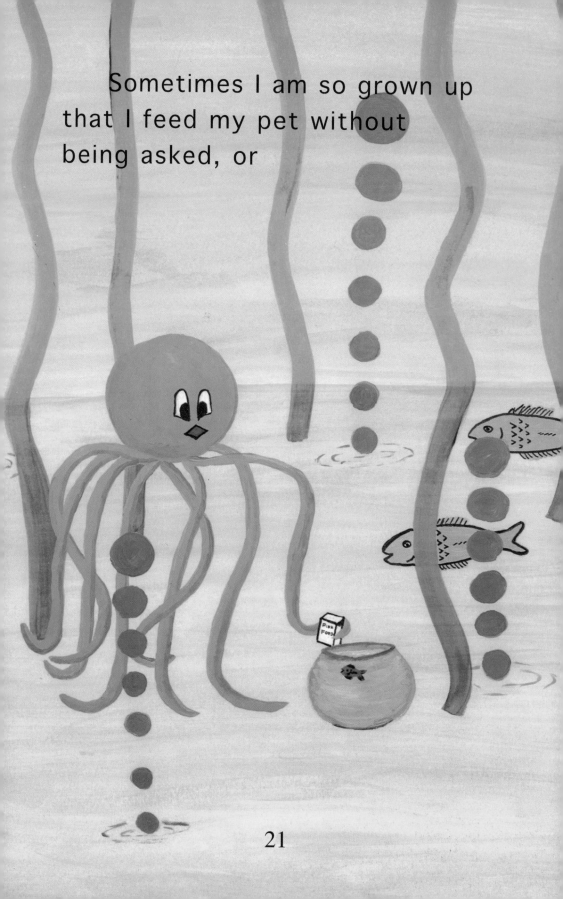

Sometimes I am so grown up
that I feed my pet without
being asked, or

21

I am so young that I want
Mommy to hold me.

Sometimes I am so smart
that I count twenty starfish, or

I am so dumb that I fish in a
teacup.

Sometimes I am so polite
that I greet my friends when
we meet, or

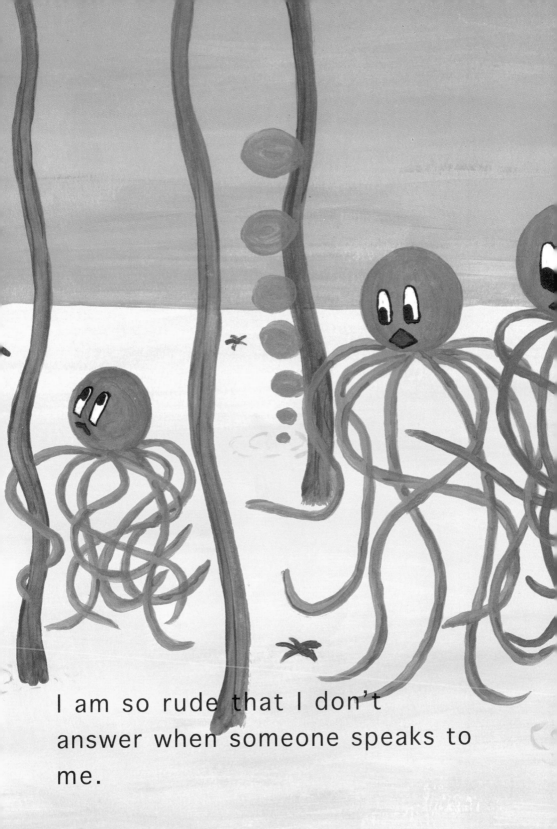

I am so rude that I don't
answer when someone speaks to
me.

Are you like this, too,
SOMETIMES?